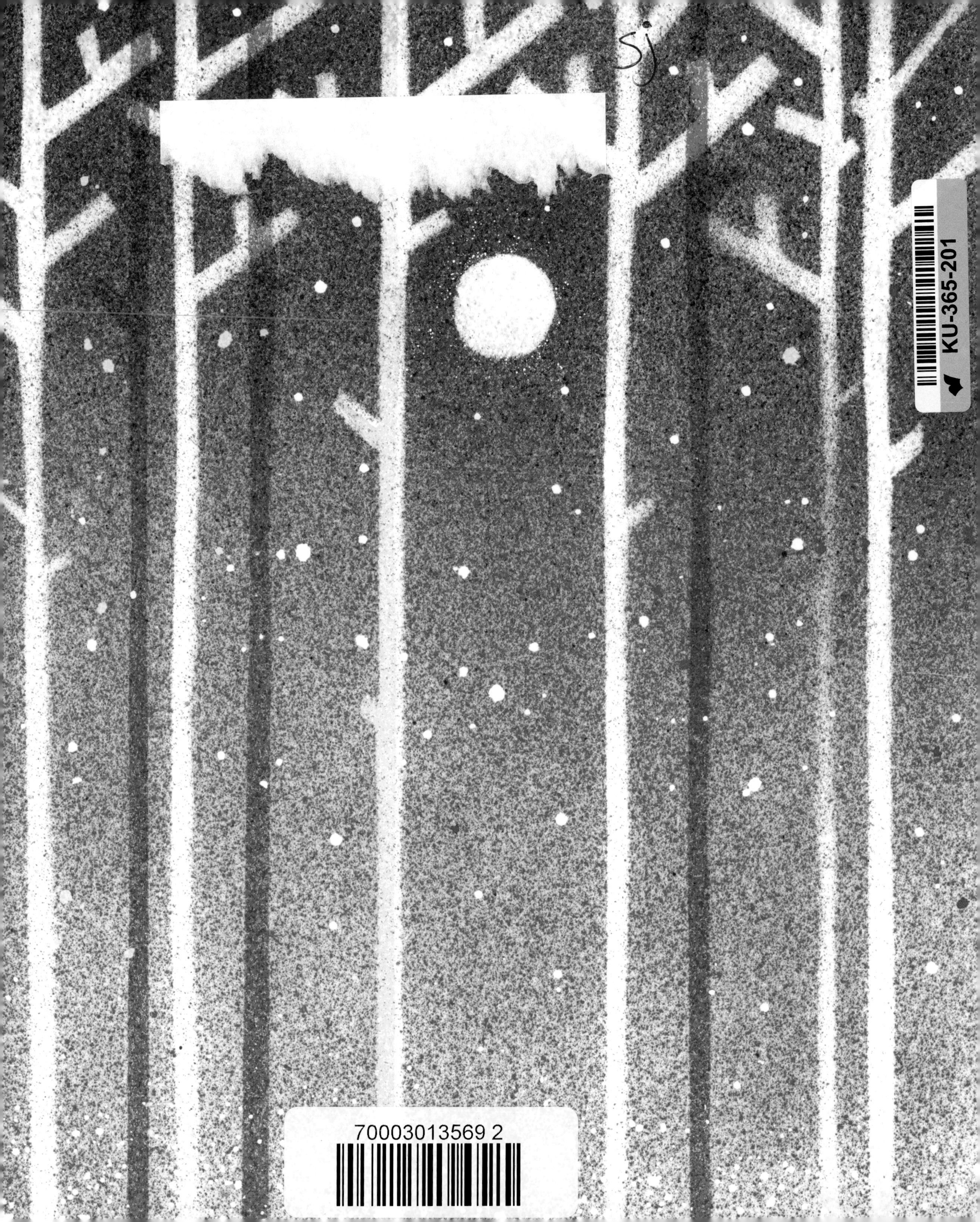

For Lettie, whose eyes are as large
and round as puddles – A.E.

Thanks to Jane, Helen and
all the S&S team – F.W.

The text in this book is an abridged version of the story,
'The Snow Dragon' by Abi Elphinstone, originally published
in the anthology *Winter Magic*.

SIMON & SCHUSTER
First published in Great Britain in 2019 by Simon & Schuster UK Ltd
1st Floor, 222 Gray's Inn Road, London WC1X 8HB • A CBS Company
Text copyright © 2016, 2019 Abi Elphinstone • Illustrations copyright ©
2019 Fiona Woodcock • The right of Abi Elphinstone and Fiona Woodcock
to be identified as the author and illustrator of this work has been asserted
by them in accordance with the Copyright, Designs and Patents Act, 1988
All rights reserved, including the right of reproduction in whole or in
part in any form • A CIP catalogue record for this book is available from
the British Library upon request • ISBN: 978-1-4711-7247-2 (HB)
ISBN: 978-1-4711-7246-5 (PB) • ISBN: 978-1-4711-7248-9 (eBook)
Printed in China • 10 9 8 7 6 5 4 3 2 1

The Snow Dragon

Abiz... (signature)

FK. Woodcock (signature)

Abi Elphinstone &
Fiona Woodcock

SIMON & SCHUSTER

London   New York   Sydney   Toronto   New Delhi

It was Christmas Eve, and Phoebe could see that the little town of Whistlethrop was covered in a thick layer of snow. It was the first snow of winter and it had come silently in the night, the way magic often does.

To Phoebe, the snow felt like a promise that today might be different from all the other days and that, just possibly, there might be even more magic waiting for her.

Phoebe lived in Griselda Bone's Home for Strays, where the strays were children and the home was, in fact, an orphanage. Once you were in, you were very firmly in.

Until Miracle Day, that was . . .

Once a month, Griselda opened the gates to parents hoping to adopt a child. If you were picked by one of the families, the day you left – that marvellous day – became your Miracle Day.

Only it never seemed to happen to Phoebe.

The pile of books Phoebe was balancing on in the attic, where she often hid away and looked out at the world, swayed and there was a scratching sound followed by a yap. A chestnut-brown sausage dog clambered up the dusty tower.

"Snow, Herb. Isn't it brilliant?" Phoebe exclaimed. But Herb was only really interested in two things: cuddles from Phoebe and dancing.

Phoebe sighed. Today was a bittersweet day. It was her friend Jack's Miracle Day.

Phoebe was happy that he was going to live with a real family, but not even Herb's pirouettes could distract her enough to forget that with Jack gone, she would be the only child left in the orphanage.

"It's just you and me now, Herb."

And then, even though she knew it was against the rules, Phoebe whispered, "Come on, if we're quick, we'll have time to wave Jack off and hurry back here before Griselda finds us."

Phoebe scooped up Herb, clambered out of the window and shimmied across the roof towards the fire escape. They hurried down the ladder and raced to the front of the orphanage, just in time to see a car pulling away. Jack looked over his shoulder and as Phoebe waved through the gates, her friend's eyes lit up.

"I'll miss you!" Jack shouted.

Phoebe stood before the tall dark gates. There was a low and very loud growl. With a sinking heart, she turned around.

A large, grumpy dog stood on the gravel. There came another growl.

"Slobber! Where have you got to?"

A woman appeared: short and stocky, with shoulders that gobbled up her neck.

Griselda peered over her clipboard at Phoebe then looked back at her register. "*Girl with hair as white as snowdrops and eyes as large and round as puddles,*" she read. "You're the one who stares at nothing through windows, aren't you?"

Phoebe shook her head. "Oh, it's never nothing, Miss Bone. There's always *something* to see."

Griselda swelled up inside her suit.

"You should know that at this orphanage, daydreaming is banned, skipping is forbidden and—"

"—hide-and-seek is out of the question," Phoebe finished glumly.

Griselda rapped her clipboard. "It is my duty to grown-ups everywhere to wage war on childishness. I will not rest until I have blasted daydreams, skipping and hide-and-seek from our country!"

Phoebe wondered where on earth all the daydreams and skipping would be banished to. Norway, perhaps?

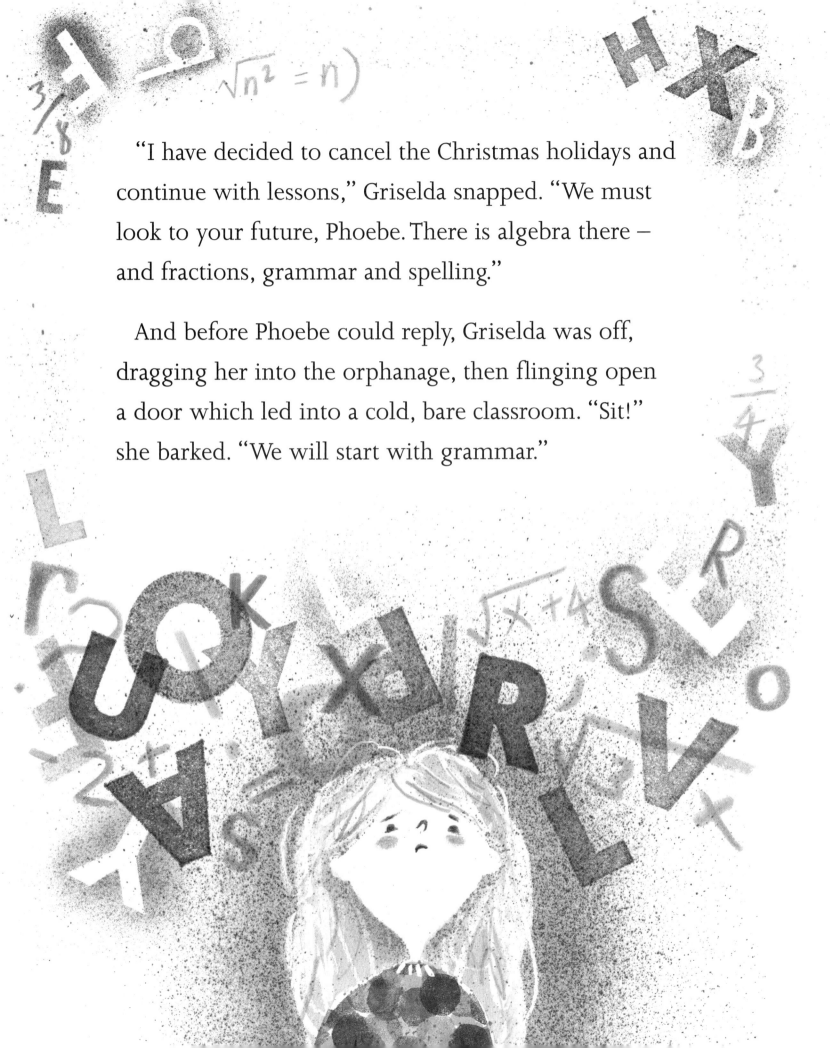

"I have decided to cancel the Christmas holidays and continue with lessons," Griselda snapped. "We must look to your future, Phoebe. There is algebra there – and fractions, grammar and spelling."

And before Phoebe could reply, Griselda was off, dragging her into the orphanage, then flinging open a door which led into a cold, bare classroom. "Sit!" she barked. "We will start with grammar."

Phoebe tried to ignore Herb's samba in the doorway and began completing the sentences in front of her.

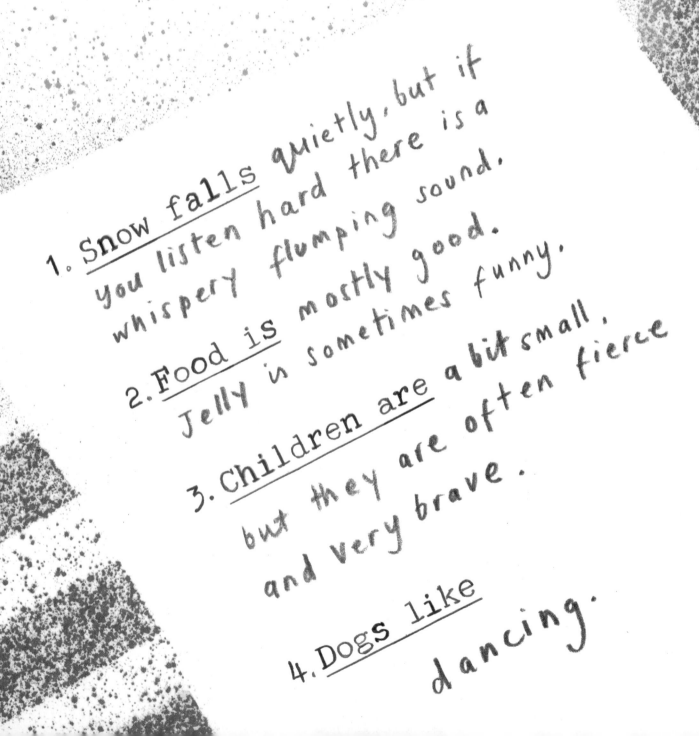

1. Snow falls quietly, but if you listen hard there is a whispery flumping sound.

2. Food is mostly good. Jelly is sometimes funny.

3. Children are a bit small, but they are often fierce and very brave.

4. Dogs like dancing.

"Excuse me," Phoebe said. "I've finished."

Griselda scanned Phoebe's sheet of paper and made a strange retching sound. "Whispery and flumping aren't even words! Dogs like DANCING?!"

Herb made a sharp exit.

"There was only one suitable response to each sentence!" Griselda boomed. "Snow falls *down*. Food is *necessary*. Children are *annoying*. And dogs like *bones!*"

Phoebe hung her head.

"You are a Word Mangler of the very worst sort.
That is the reason nobody wants to adopt you.
Only a night in the kennels will drive this childishness
out of you!"

Phoebe tried to protest, but Griselda and Slobber
were already marching her outside. Griselda flung
Phoebe into a kennel and fastened a metal cuff around
her ankle, before striding away with Slobber at her
pinstriped heels.

Phoebe sniffed as a tear smudged down her nose,
so Herb scampered inside the kennel, performed
a hopeful little waltz, then snuggled into her chest.
And while families laughed and sang and played
beyond the orphanage walls, Phoebe and Herb
watched their Christmas Eve drain away.

But then, tiny white flecks
started falling
from the
sky.

"It's snowing, Herb! I reckon this chain's long enough for me to climb outside . . . We could build a snowman!"

They rolled a ball of snow back and forth, and after a while, Phoebe stood back and beamed. "He's like a guardian, Herb – someone to watch out for us this Christmas." She paused. "He's possibly a little bit magical, too."

And as the girl and the sausage dog looked, they had the strangest feeling that maybe there *was* something more to their guardian than first met the eye . . .

Hours passed and Phoebe lay shivering in the kennel. Then, just as she was about to fall asleep, a movement caught her eye. It was nothing much – only the feeling of an image half glimpsed.

When Phoebe looked again though, she saw that something extraordinary was happening.

The snowman was changing. Ribbons of snow were twisting free and spinning in the air until they rose before the kennel in a swirl of glittering silver.

"It – it can't be . . ." Phoebe whispered.

Right there in the grounds of the orphanage was a dragon – and its snow-carved body glinted in the moonlight.

Then the dragon spoke. His voice was soft and feathery and he simply said: "Hello."

"Hello," Phoebe found herself replying. "I'm Phoebe, and this is Herb."

The dragon wiggled his enormous ears. "What fine names for adventurers."

Phoebe's chest swelled and Herb did a quick cancan. "We're going on an adventure?"

The dragon nodded. "Dragons only appear to those who need them. We stay for one adventure and then we melt back into the landscape." He smiled. "I suggest we set off. You can be late for many things in life, but you should never keep an adventure waiting."

Phoebe's eyes grew large because that was quite possibly the best sentence anyone had ever said to her.

As the dragon spoke, the cuff around Phoebe's ankle clicked open and a white cloak appeared around her shoulders.

The dragon lowered his body and Phoebe climbed carefully up his leg, before settling herself and Herb just below his ears.

"Do you know why my ears are so large?" the dragon whispered. Phoebe shook her head. "So I can listen to all of the wonderful things that you have to say."

Phoebe's heart glowed. There might be a woman in pinstripe trying to tear her down, but here was a dragon, building her up.

The dragon lumbered forward. One stride and he was over the gravel, another and he was past the flower beds, and just as Phoebe thought they would career into the trees, he surged into the sky.

Up and up they went!

"We're flying, Herb!" Phoebe cried. She looked down at the streets below and noticed a gap in somebody's bedroom curtains. Two children were sitting up late on a bed and in between them was an unopened present. But when Phoebe peered more closely, she saw they were snatching the present back and forth. Phoebe frowned. "Why are they fighting, Snow Dragon?"

"They do not realize how lucky they are," the dragon replied. "They are always wanting more, but everything they could ever want is right there already."

The dragon raced on over country lanes dusted with snow and lakes locked in the cold, hard gleam of ice.

"What do you like best in the world, Phoebe?" the dragon asked.

Herb gave a little bark from her lap. "Other than Herb," Phoebe said, "I love trees. And mountains, though I've only seen them in books. And I think the sea looks very promising, too."

The dragon chuckled. "We'll go north, then, where the forests are bigger, the mountains are higher and the seas are deeper."

And north they went, the dragon's wings shredding through the pearly night. He dived over a forest, breaking just before the canopy, and Phoebe stuck out her arm to grab a fistful of snow. She smiled. Here she was, on the back of a dragon, exploring an untouched kingdom of snow and ice.

"We're like birds, Herb! As free and as fast as birds!" They sailed over a train rushing through the countryside and Phoebe gasped as she took in the carriages of people. "What happens if we're seen, Snow Dragon?"

"Oh, we won't be seen." The dragon's voice was soft and low. "We all have the gift of wonder, Phoebe. But sometimes we forget how to take a good, long look at the world and so we miss the miracles all around us."
Phoebe stroked Herb. "I won't ever forget."

They flew on to the mountains where the summits reached up and touched the sky.

The dragon circled the highest peak and then sank lower, until his talons crunched onto the mountaintop. He folded his great wings in and they sat, without saying a word, the whole world spread out below them.

Then, into the silence, the sky began to change. Strands of green shimmered between stars and then waves of purple rolled through, sending new shades twirling across the sky.

"It's the Northern Lights, isn't it?" Phoebe swallowed in disbelief. "Would you mind if I howled? It's just all so – wonderflible!"

The dragon's wings twitched and Phoebe suddenly worried that he was annoyed she had accidentally mangled another word. But the dragon only smiled.

"I was thinking just the same thing. Howling on three?"

Phoebe nodded, then she emptied her lungs into the mountains and the sky, and the dragon howled and Herb barked. And for a few minutes, it was just the three of them, sending their voices out into the wilderness as if they were a part of the ice and the rock and the swirl of colours around them.

Then the dragon rubbed his head gently against
Phoebe and though she tried to stifle her yawn, it
squeaked out. He pushed off from the crag and they
skimmed over mountains, glens and castles until they
were whizzing above the silver sea. The dragon's talons
tore through the surface and Phoebe swung a hand
down to touch the water so that she would remember,
days later when she was trapped in the orphanage,
that she had ridden a snow dragon over the North Sea.

"Happy Christmas, dear Phoebe," the dragon whispered.
Phoebe ruffled his ragged ears. "Happy Christmas,
Snow Dragon. It's been the best one of my life!"

Herb did a celebratory jig on her lap and then
they sat watchfully as the dragon glided back over
the countryside.

The stars were still shining when they touched down
in front of the kennel, and Phoebe wondered whether
any time had passed at all.

"Thank you," she said as she slid down the dragon's leg, "for the adventure and the talking and all the other bits in between."

Phoebe wrapped her arms around the dragon's neck and he closed his wings over her. After a while, he drew back but as he did, he spoke in a rumbling whisper.

"Some day your life will open up, far beyond these orphanage walls, and when it does, Phoebe, I want you to remember our adventure.

Be content.

Be watchful.

Be brave.

And never stop believing in miracles."

The snow before Phoebe began to shift and swirl then the dragon faded. Phoebe's cloak vanished, too, and she felt the metal cuff around her ankle again. She turned to Herb, and together they traipsed back towards the kennel, to dream of skies that danced with colour and mountains cast in ice.

The next morning, Phoebe woke to the sound of footsteps and soon Griselda came into view.

"Slobber and I were mulling over our latest policy for the War Against Childishness. It's called: 'How To Stamp Out Word Mangling'." She glared at Phoebe whose teeth were chattering. "What do you think?"

Phoebe tried to conjure up the Snow Dragon in her thoughts. His magic had made her feel important but now a horrible emptiness spread out inside her. She took a deep breath as she remembered the dragon's words and willed herself to be brave.

"Happy Christmas, Miss Bone."

"Christmas?!"

Griselda ground the word between her teeth. Then she threw Phoebe a dark smile.

"I had forgotten about our Christmas Chase – the only thing that makes this dreadful day even slightly bearable."

Phoebe shuddered. The Chase was a miserable event which saw Griselda and Slobber pursuing the children through the orphanage until Slobber found the juicy bones they were told to clutch.

"I had thought there wouldn't be a Chase this year with all the orphans gone," Griselda sniggered. "But Miracle Day didn't come to everybody, did it?"
Phoebe shook her head.

Griselda performed several squats, then she wrenched the cuff from Phoebe's ankle. Minutes later, Phoebe was crouching at the top of the stairs, a bone clasped tight in her hand.

Griselda's whistle blared through the house and Phoebe's whole body trembled.

"Run!" Griselda yelled.

Phoebe and Herb tore down the stairs, before skidding into the hall and racing towards the grandfather clock. They clambered inside it and pulled the door closed behind them.

Outside, paintings crashed to the floor and furniture toppled. Phoebe squeezed her eyes shut as she thought of the Snow Dragon's words: *Some day your life will open up.* Phoebe wished that day closer. *Let it be now. Let it be today.*

"To the attic!" Griselda yelled to Slobber. They ran from the hall, smashing vases and tearing down lamps, and so it was perhaps unsurprising that they didn't hear the doorbell ring. But Phoebe heard it, and a flicker of hope stirred inside her. Quietly, carefully, she pushed the grandfather clock open and tiptoed towards the door. Then, hoping so hard that her toes curled up inside her shoes, she turned the handle.

A man and a woman stood before her. The woman had long brown hair and a smile so full of warmth and kindness that Phoebe felt her knees wobble. She looked at the man beside her whose hair was also dark but whose eyes were as bright and blue as his scarf.

The Chase raged on as Griselda and Slobber clattered along the corridors, but the couple didn't seem interested in any of that.

"We received some paperwork this morning," the woman said, holding up a file. "These are the legal documents for the adoption of a seven-year-old girl with hair as white as snowdrops and eyes as large and round as puddles." Phoebe's heart fluttered. "It's you – isn't it? The child we've always been hoping for?"

Phoebe stayed very still and very silent. She didn't want to ruin the most exciting conversation she had ever had.

"The documents are signed by a lawyer from a firm called Snowdon Dragonis," said the man. "And," he glanced behind him, "although the orphanage was locked, we climbed over the gates anyway because we knew – because we hoped – that you might be inside."

Phoebe shut her eyes for a few seconds and then opened them again, half expecting the couple to have disappeared. But they were still there and the paperwork was still there and the possibility that she might be wanted and loved – that was still there, too.

Her Miracle Day had come.

And it was more wonderful and more magical than anything she could have dared to hope for.

"I'm Phoebe," she said quietly. "And this is Herb."

And while Griselda and Slobber stormed through the orphanage, the man, the woman, the sausage dog and the seven-year-old girl with hair as white as snowdrops and eyes as large and round as puddles climbed over the padlocked gates and walked out into the world.